Samantha

ELLEN STOLL WALSH

HARCOURT BRACE & COMPANY

San Diego   New York   London

Library of Congress Cataloging-in-Publication Data
Walsh, Ellen Stoll.
Samantha/Ellen Stoll Walsh.
p.   cm.
Summary: Samantha, the smallest of the mouse
children, wants a fairy godmother to protect her from
her rougher brothers and sisters.
ISBN 0-15-252264-6
[1. Brothers and sisters—Fiction. 2. Fairies—Fiction. 3.
Mice—Fiction.]   I. Title.
PZ7.W1675Sam   1996
[E]—dc20   95-12809

First edition   A B C D E

Printed in Singapore

The illustrations in this book are cut-paper collage.
The display type was set in Phyllis and Lithos Black.
The text type was set in Adroit Light.
Color separations by Bright Arts, Ltd., Singapore
Printed and bound by Tien Wah Press, Singapore
This book was printed with soya-based inks on
Leykam recycled paper, which contains more than
20 percent postconsumer waste and has a total
recycled content of at least 50 percent.
Production supervision by Warren Wallerstein
and David Hough
Designed by Camilla Filancia

For my nieces and nephews—Laura,
Rena, David, Michele, Megan,
Howard, Betsy, Joe, Demian,
Max, and Jomar

Of all the mouse children, Samantha was the smallest. Sometimes her brothers and sisters were a bit too rough.

And oh, how they could tease.

"What I need," said Samantha, "is a fairy godmother for protection."

A fairy godmother must have been listening, because one appeared out of nowhere to take up her new responsibilities.

Before long Samantha's fairy godmother was like a member of the family.

When the mouse children went out to play, Samantha and her fairy godmother went, too.

But they stayed quietly out of the way.

"Come and play with us," said the mouse children.
"No!" said Samantha. "I'm staying right here!"

"Watch me run, Samantha," her brothers and sisters called. "Watch me jump!"

Samantha was pretty sure she could run and jump as well as they could, and she was tempted to try, but she wasn't ready to take any chances.

Until one day it rained, and Samantha felt like running and shouting and getting wet with the others. Instead, her fairy godmother kept her dry, while her brothers and sisters danced and pretended to melt.

And when at last it snowed, not one flake landed on Samantha.

It wasn't fair! Samantha wanted to play in that white, wonderful softness with her brothers and sisters.

Before she could stop herself she shouted, "Just go away!" to her fairy godmother.

Samantha was sorry for what she had said, but soon forgot all about it because she was having so much fun.

She could hardly wait to tell her fairy godmother what fun she'd had. But when she arrived home cold and wet and tired and happy, her fairy godmother wasn't there.

Samantha set out early the next morning to find her.

Fresh snow made everything look unfamiliar, and before long she was lost. But her fairy godmother wasn't lost.

She was watching.

When Samantha fell into a drift, her fairy godmother
floated down and helped her out.

"I see you still need me a little," she said.

"I need you a lot," said Samantha. "But from now on, Fairy Godmother, you might be safer if you don't get quite so close when I play."

And ever after that, Samantha's fairy godmother sat at a safe distance and watched Samantha take her chances with the other mouse children.